Hush, Mama Loves You

Hush, Mama Loves You

Anna Strauss

illustrated by Alice Priestley

Walker & Company
New York

For Mom, Dad, and David Reed.
Special thanks to my friends and neighbors
who helped through the many stages of the book. – A. S.

In memory of my grandparents. – A. P.

First published in the United States of America in 2002 by
Walker Publishing Company, Inc.

Published in Canada in 2002 by Key Porter Books Limited.
Designed by Peter Maher

For information about permission to reproduce selections from
this book, write to Permissions, Walker & Company, 435 Hudson Street, New York, New York 10014

Library of Congress Cataloging-in-Publication Data
available upon request

ISBN 0-8027-8806-8 (hardcover)
ISBN 0-8027-8807-6 (reinforced)

Printed in Singapore

2 4 6 8 10 9 7 5 3 1

Sara was a happy little girl who loved to play outside.

She would swing on swings,

slide down slides,

and even climb trees.

Sometimes she would fall down and hurt herself.

Her mother would take her in her arms and say,

"Close your eyes, my baby. This too shall pass. Hush the hurt, my heart. Tears may fall but I am here, so hush."

This always made Sara feel much better.

She would give her mom a BIG hug

and go back to playing.

When it was time for Sara's first day of school, she was very nervous.

To make her feel better, Sara's mom made her a yummy lunch.

She also held her hand all the way to school.

At school, one of the girls yanked Sara's ponytail.

Sara ran home crying.

Her mother took her in her arms and said,

Close your eyes, my baby.
This too shall pass.
Hush
the hurt,
my heart.
Tears may fall but
I am here,
so hush.

The next day Sara told the hair-puller that she'd hurt her feelings.

At recess the two girls played together.

Sara usually did well at school. One day, in fifth grade, she failed a math test.

She ran home and her mother gathered her in her arms and said the words that always made her feel better.

Close your eyes, my baby. This too shall pass. Hush —the hurt, my heart. Tears may fall but I am here, so hush.

Sara smiled and gave her mom a BIG hug.

When the next math test came along, Sara and her mother studied together.

Sara got a B on that test

and then an A on the next.

Years passed, and Sara became a teenager. She wore strange clothes and said mean things, just to upset her mother.

One day she went to a party and met a boy.

They swung on swings,

slid down slides,

and even climbed trees.
They fell in love.

Then the boy had to move to Australia. He promised to write every day, but he only wrote once.

Sara cried until the room was filled with her tears. Her mother said,

Close your eyes, my baby.
This too shall pass.
Hush the hurt, my heart.
Tears may fall but I am here, so hush.

Then she told Sara about her first boyfriend. Sara smiled and gave her mom a BIG hug. Then she went outside and talked about boys with her friends.

Sara grew up even more and moved away from her mother.

She got married

and had Natalie,
a little girl
of her own.

One day Natalie ran home crying because a boy
had put gum in her hair. Sara cut out the icky gum
and then, remembering the words her mother used
to say, she took her daughter in her arms and said,

Close your eyes, my baby.
This too shall pass.
Hush the hurt, my heart.
Tears may fall but I am here,
so hush.

Natalie smiled and gave her mom a BIG hug. Then she went outside to show off her new short hair.

They swung on swings.

They slid down
slides.

They even tried to
climb a tree, but couldn't.
Instead, they all fell down laughing
and laughed all the way home.

When the time came for Sara's mother to leave, Natalie began to cry.

Sara and her mother took her in their arms and said,

Close your eyes, my baby.

This too shall pass.

Hush the hurt, my heart.

Tears may fall but I am here, so hush.